THE RIGHT TO
BECOME

JOYCELYN OGUNSOLA

right -

/rīt/

(noun)

1. That which is due to anyone by just claim, legal guarantees or moral principles.

"I have the right to become everything that Jesus died for me to become."

Synonyms: entitlement, privilege, birthright, liberty, license, consent, authority, permission.

"But to all who believed him and accepted him, he gave the right to become children of God."

John 1:12

"He made the one who did not know sin to be sin for us, so that in him we might become the righteousness of God"

2nd Corinthians 5:12

INTRODUCTION

I believe that there is freedom found in vulnerability. I believe that vulnerability bridges the gap to connectivity, and I believe that connectivity fosters an environment for people to be open and transparent. This is exactly what I aim to do with this book. My purpose in writing this book is to be as honest, as real, as raw, and as transparent as I can be so that you can glean from my story and find the strength to seek out your own healing, deliverance and freedom that can only be found in Christ Jesus.

So here it goes folks, journey with me through the chapters of this book as we discover how the redemptive work of the cross has made a way for me to become.

JOYCELYN OGUNSOLA

TABLE OF CONTENTS

1. The Hider & The Seeker   8

2. The Beginning of a Lie   42

3. My Biggest Failure   53

4. Becoming God's Woman   79

5. Into His Marvelous Light   106

JOYCELYN OGUNSOLA

1

The Hider & The Seeker

Growing up, "Hide-And-Go-Seek" was the only game that I was a true mastermind at. My siblings and I used to play it all the time. If I wasn't playing house or dress-up with my sister, it was "Hide-And-Go-Seek". In the game, there are usually one or more hiders and there is always one seeker. As the game commences, the seeker is the one who closes his or her eyes as they count to a certain predetermined number (our number was always 50). We played fair and the seeker always gave the hiders an ample amount of time to hide.

The pressure was always on as the hiders scurry along the house to find a suitable hiding place where it would be almost impossible for them to be found. *"...45...46...47...48...49...50!!! Ready or not here I come!"* The seeker stops counting and suddenly, all you hear is complete silence. As the hiders are snuggled up in their various hiding places, the seeker, like a hungry lion looking for prey to catch, goes out to seek those who are hiding.

But the key to the game is to never be found. That's the object of the game. The hiders hide and the seeker seeks. Many children grow up playing this game for fun, but I found that not only was I playing the game, I was living in the game. I was always the hider, not just in "Hide-And-Go-Seek" but in real life. I hid from my friends, parents, siblings, social media, the world, and yes even from God. And get this, I was good at it too!

Whenever the doorbell would ring, I would be the last one to oblige to answer it because I didn't want to be seen. I always felt that opening the door and inviting people in was an invasion of my privacy. I was inviting the outsiders into my world and that was always something that I greatly feared. Whenever my family members came over to visit, I would always dread the feeling of leaving my room go downstairs to greet them (and being a Nigerian-American didn't help at all). If any of my relatives found out that I was home while they came to visit (completely unannounced and unexpected may I add) and I didn't bother to greet them, they would come for my neck and my head.

For me to avoid all the potential drama that would arise, I would stay in my room and pretend that I was sleeping. The age-old trick. But I quickly learned that that 'trick' was getting too old after my parents stopped falling for it and realized that just because my lights were turned off and the comforter was pulled over my head it doesn't mean that I was really asleep. So, what did I do in lieu of this? I opted to find new hiding places.

Since my bedroom wasn't safe enough, I tried my closet. My sister and I shared a room growing up but when she moved out of state for college, our space became my space even though she left behind a few of her belongings. I, I mean *we* had a very long and narrow closet that was filled with about 95% of my own belongings that comprised of clothes, hampers, a huge trash bag of shoes and a box filled with my ever-growing book collection so there were ample of things for me to hide behind.

Growing up in a Nigerian household, hushed tones were never a thing. I distinctly remember a time when my parents had guests over and how I could hear boisterous laughter booming through the entire house. It felt as if each guest brought their outside voice inside and it never switched off for that entire night. Africans are loud and they know it. But not only are they loud and well-aware, they simply just don't care.

Somehow, over the thunderous laughs that could shake Mount Kilimanjaro and the booming voices that sounded like they had a built-in megaphone, I barely managed to hear that I had an incoming phone-call from my little brother. Assuming that this call would consist of him telling me that the aunties and uncles (as we would always refer to them as, not Mr. or Mrs.) that came to visit our parents were asking for me and wanted to see me, fear immediately sprang up within me. I completely ignored my ringing phone and I retreated to hiding behind my box of books and long evening gowns that I stored in my closet.

The incoming call stopped, and I was now safe and secure in my hiding place. But all of a sudden, I heard the sound of my little brother's footsteps coming up the steps (because when you've lived with someone your entire life you learn the sound of their footsteps) and my heart began to palpitate fiercely inside of my chest for fear that I might be found. My little brother was looking for me because to his understanding I didn't leave the house and the only place that I would likely be in is my bedroom.

As I heard his footsteps approach the door of my room, I tried to remain quiet while anxiously trying to turn the ringer volume of my phone to silent just in case he thinks to call me again. Moments later, I hear the doorknob twist open as he walks in and takes a pause in his steps. In the middle of his pause, I couldn't make out whether he let out a sigh or a deep breath once he realized that I wasn't in my room.

But to my terrifying surprise, he flung open the door of the closet in my room as if he knew that he might find me there.

Scared that I would possibly be found and embarrassed that my own brother would be the one to do so, I remained as quiet as a mouse and didn't flinch a muscle. After he didn't see my petite 5'3 frame, I heard him close the door of my closet and walk out of my bedroom into another room. I stayed scrunched up behind my box of books and long evening gowns for a good fifteen minutes just to make sure that the coast was clear. He came back within those fifteen minutes, but when he found that things were the same as he left them, he gave up.

Glad that I made the decision to hide out a little longer and relieved that he never found me, I finally felt free enough to come out of my hiding place. But I didn't come out alone, I came out with various thoughts that probed my mind. *Closets were not made for people; they were made for storage and clothes, so I wondered what made my little brother think to even open my closet? Did he think that he could potentially find me there? What if he found me? The cat would have been let out of the bag. My secret would have been revealed.*

The only thing that was keeping me from being found were the box of books and long evening gowns that I hid behind. All he had to do was pull those dresses back and shift the box and my fearful face would have been seen. *I wonder what he would say. I wonder what he would think. I wonder what he would do.* Regardless of those thoughts, I was glad that he never pulled back those beautiful gowns to see the ugliness of my insecurity that came with my hiding.

MORE HIDING PLACES

My bedroom and my closet were not my only hiding places. Whenever my parents weren't around, I hid in their room, I hide in the basement and I even hid in the garage. But I knew that I couldn't lock myself in my room or my parent's house forever because I still had to go to school and do other regular mundane things that human beings needed to do. Whenever I left my parent's house and stepped out into "the outside world", the dark abyss, the place where I felt the most vulnerable and seen, I would discover new hiding places. I hid in the bathroom stalls at school. I hid at the park (*I know, I know, you're probably wondering how but trust me I found my own little special hiding place*). I hid in the library. I hid at the mall. I hid anywhere that I could.

I got so good at hiding that no one really knew where I was or even *who* I was for that matter. No one knew what I liked to do, what my favorite color was or if I even had a favorite color (I don't). No one knew how many siblings I had, whether my father was of a lighter complexion or a darker complexion, not even the people that I called my close friends. No one knew what made me laugh from the depths of my belly or what made me cry myself to sleep every night for several years. Nobody knew because I didn't allow them to know. I didn't want them to know. You see, I wanted to be invisible. I was content with not being known, not being popular, not having many friends and people not knowing who I was. I was okay with being a mediocre student because I was too afraid that if I knew the right answer to a question and I raised my hand that the teacher would call on me and make me share my response in front of the entire class. I was okay with getting grades that didn't require extreme recognition because getting Principal's Honor Roll would mean that I would be known as the girl who got "Straight A's".

Becoming the valedictorian or salutatorian of my graduating high-school class meant that I would have to give a speech and sit on the stage with the other superintendents of the school and that required for all eyes to be on me. I never pursued reaching for the top because I knew that being at the top meant that you had to be seen and being seen meant that you had to be heard and being heard meant that people had to stop and take notice of you. And I wanted absolutely nothing to do with anything that required for me to be seen, heard or noticed.

I wanted to live a life of mediocrity because it was safe. I thought that if I just did enough in school to get by, I would be just fine. If I showed up to the church event just so that I can say that I was there but don't stay after to fellowship with anyone so no one would ask me questions pertaining to my spiritual life, I would be fine. Every time I left the house, it was a risk that I was putting myself in—a risk to be vulnerable. I always wanted to hurry up, get out of the space where people saw me so that I could hurry home, crawl back into my cave and hide.

FEAR BECAME MY GOD

Being introverted aided in this defense mechanism a lot. Naturally, I enjoy being by myself. I enjoy my own company, but my introverted instincts fueled my desire to isolate myself and hide. Away from my family, away from my friends, away from people, away from the world and away from God. Just me, myself, and I... or *so I thought.*

I grew up in a home where I was taught to not trust people. I was taught to never tell anyone my secrets and to always keep to myself because if I dare open my mouth and share the ugliest parts of me then someone might use it against me. My introverted tendencies and the way that I grew up affirmed my hiding. It made hiding okay. It made hiding acceptable because it was deemed as my normal. But I realized that just because something is considered the norm for you doesn't necessarily make that thing okay. Just because it's normal for you to steal money out of your mom's purse every Friday doesn't mean that it's okay. Just because it's normal for you to constantly have lustful thoughts about women doesn't mean that it's okay. I quickly learned that what I considered to be 'my norm' was simply just a response to my trauma and my dysfunction and God wasn't pleased with it. He didn't like the fact that I was hiding.

PAUSE. I want you to stop and ask yourself this question: What thing have you considered as 'a norm' in your life that you know isn't deemed acceptable in the eyes of God?

I became comfortable in my dysfunction and I was living in my own little world with me being the only occupant and I thought everything was okay because I was the only civilian. I was viewing everything from such a broken and twisted perspective. I was viewing men, women, the world, sex, God, relationships, family and myself all from broken lenses. I was viewing everything outside of the world that I had created for myself as dangerous and I didn't want to be a part of what wasn't safe. I believed that the only sense of safety that I could experience was within myself, so I looked to myself for protection and safety.

I didn't look to men because from my experiences, I was taught that men were dangerous and that they were never to be trusted. I didn't look to my family because there was so much dysfunction and I thought no one would understand. I didn't look to friendships because I didn't know how to be open to any friend without disclosing too much information. I didn't look to God because

I felt that He was so distant and wanted absolutely nothing to do with a broken little girl like me.

But not only did I look to myself, I looked to food, I looked to shopping and I looked to books for safety and comfort as well. These things, though strange and uncommon were also hiding places for me. The comfort that these things brought me only lasted but a moment until I found myself hiding in another closet, reaching for another bowl of jellof rice (carbs were my weakness), browsing on another online website or reading another book that would potentially take the place of my personal study of God's Word.

Yes, I found hiding places even after I found Christ and the things that I looked to for safety are no different from turning to pornography, drugs, masturbation, alcohol, a man or a woman. They all share a commonality in the sense that each one of these things all have the propensity to take the place of God in your heart.

There have been countless and countless of times where I have chosen fear over God and I allowed the sinful desires of my heart to win and when I realized that it wasn't satisfying, I came back for more comfort. All the while I never even wondered how God was feeling. His Word tells me that He is a jealous God, not jealous in the sense of wanting what I have, but jealous in the sense of wanting me...*all* of me. But I was always afraid of giving Him all of me because I knew that that required a level of unmasking and unveiling that I wasn't ready for.

Every moment that I stepped outside of my little world into the "real world", I would always find myself in a trance. I always believed it to be just regular daydreaming and that it was normal, but I soon realized that the "trance" that I would find myself in wasn't normal and that it was much deeper than an innocent daydream. It was a portal that I opened. It was a place where I allowed fear to come in and dine with me. Every time I opened that portal I was no longer living in my present reality; I was in a completely different world—a world that I was being pulled into by my own fears. And each day this world became my sunken reality.

THE RIGHT TO BECOME

Every time I opened this portal, it felt like I was being hypnotized by fear and fear offered me something that no one else ever did; it offered me protection and safety. Fear said that if I just stayed put and never came out of my hypnosis then I would be safe. I would be protected. The offer was enticing, and I always accepted it because I never felt safe within the "real world". Everything in the real world was scary; the thought of letting people in, becoming vulnerable, allowing myself to be seen and known by people was sickening so I continued to open the portals in my mind and allowed it to take me to a place of safety.

Every time people came around, I hid. I didn't want to be anywhere that people were. I didn't want them to see me. I didn't want them to look me in my eyes and I didn't want them to know who I was because I was afraid. I was terrified of being vulnerable, of being seen, heard, desired, wanted and noticed by both men and women so I continued to hide.

THE FOOTBALL PLAYER

In high school, there was a football player who really liked me. I mean, he *wanted* me, and he made it known not only to me, but to his teammates and friends that it was me that he wanted. But I, on the other hand, wanted absolutely nothing to do with him. I tried my best to hide from him and not pay him any mind, but he never seemed to pick up on the hints that I was dropping him. Me distancing myself away from him didn't seem to be enough and all the while I just couldn't see what he saw in me. I didn't understand why he wanted to be with me so badly because it's not like I wanted to be with him.

Several years later, I now understand that I was being blinded by my own insecurities. It was my insecurities that didn't allow me to see what that football player saw in me. He thought I was beautiful, I thought I was completely unattractive. He said things like, *"I've never met a girl like you before",* but I never fell for his sweet nothings even though everything inside of my young feminine heart wanted to.

I never allowed myself to feel the emotion of a man's love for me. I was afraid of the attention that he gave me, and I knew that if I received him and allowed him to romance me then that would potentially put me in a position to be called a football player's girlfriend and I didn't want that. I didn't want him. I didn't want the title. I didn't want the attention. I didn't want the stares. I didn't want the whispers. I didn't want the looks and glances. I didn't want any of it.

THE MISSING FRAMED PICTURE

I hated taking pictures because not only did I not deem myself as attractive, I just didn't like seeing an image of myself practically anywhere. I was never comfortable in front of a camera. I was always afraid to take pictures because I knew that I would never like what I would see.

If you visit my parents' house, there are pictures in the living room of my parents and my siblings but none of me. There was this framed picture of me that my parents mounted on the wall that I absolutely hated but to anyone that came over and visited it was perfect and it gave the living room a beautiful aesthetic. The lineup was beautiful as well, it was a picture of me, a picture of my parents and then a picture of my sister. One day, I looked at that picture completely disgusted with myself at how I looked so I took it down and hid it. Of course, my very Nigerian mother was upset when she saw the vacancy on the wall, so she summoned me to go find it, but I never did. To this day I still have no idea where that picture is, and I'll be honest with myself and with you and say that I'm glad that I never found it.

My high-school graduation was an interesting day. I wasn't happy but my parents were. I took pictures but I didn't want to. I have tw o great friends of mine that graduated the same year as me and to this day they still jokingly question if I ever graduated from high school because they never saw my graduation pictures. I took the pictures, but I never showed them to anyone.

THE BEGINNING OF IT ALL - CIRCA 2007

At this point, you may be wondering, where did this hiding thing originate from? Where did it all begin for me? And of all the things that I could possibly want in the world, why did I desperately crave protection and safety?

Well, let's take a trip down memory lane, shall we?

All of elementary school up until 6th grade was honestly a blur for me but there was one distinct memory that happened during my elementary school days that completely distorted the way that I viewed life. My dad used to take my siblings and I to our local library almost every day after school. Ever since I can remember, I have always had a deep love for reading so I always looked forward to our trips to the library. Everything about the library fascinated me; from the number of books that were on the shelves, to the different genres that were displayed, to even the smell of paper inside of the books. Being at the library was a true happy place for me.

My dad always had some sort of work to do whenever we arrived, so he allowed us to be free to roam around the library fishing for books (age appropriate of course) to check-out and take home. But there was one day that I remember that completely changed my whole library experience.

One scorching hot day after school, we rode to the library and once we arrived, I hopped out of the car, instantly took off, ran straight into the library and started browsing through the bookshelves so eager to see what new read I could find. In the middle of me browsing through the shelves, I noticed that a man, who was a stranger, was following me. And of course, like any sensible child would, I got a little worried, so I ran back to my dad who was busy working and said to him," Daddy, *I think that man is following me.*" At this point the man that I claimed to have been following me was visible to my father, so I was able to point out exactly which man I was referring to. My dad looked up and locked eyes with the man that I referred to, waved at him and said, *"Oh, he's not following you. I think he just knows me."*

After that, the man walked away, and my dad returned to finish up whatever he was working on. So, I believed that everything was fine and that maybe this strange man did know who my father was and that I looked familiar to him so I too, returned to what I was doing. I continued in my quest for books, but nothing seemed to stand out to me. Suddenly, the same man appeared again and this time he was in the same aisle of books that I was in. I was on one side of the bookshelf and he was on the opposite side.

We weren't in close proximity, but we were close enough for him to see that I was a little girl and for me to see that he was a grown man. He locked eyes with me and gave me a blank stare as if he were waiting to capture my attention. I stood there waiting to see if he was going to say anything, but he mustered no words to me. While he had my attention, he used it to his best advantage, he didn't walk over to me, but he did something that left me scarred, confused and believing that men were the most dangerous group of species on the planet from that day on.

He groped his private area and he smiled while doing it. It was like the sight of a little girl aroused his sexual interest and when he was done, he walked away. He walked away satisfied and I walked away confused and vulnerable. After that moment in my life, everything became blurry. I no longer saw men the same. I no longer felt safe and protected around the presence of a man. I felt like that strange man took something that I could no longer get back. He took my vulnerability and he completely defamed any positive outlook of masculinity that I had.

Men became a danger zone for me. I no longer trusted people and I felt like I had to constantly protect myself not because I wanted to but because I had to. That day, in the car ride home, I made an inner vow that said I will never allow myself to be vulnerable again and that was the beginning of my hiding.

THE RIGHT TO FREEDOM

It wasn't until years after I got saved that I realized that I was living in bondage and that my way of thinking was completely twisted. Yes, even after you receive salvation it is still possible for you to live in bondage. Think of the people of Israel. All throughout scripture God stamped, declared and announced that Israel was His son. God declared that Israel was His very own possession and that they belonged to Him. But even after God set them free from the hand of the Egyptians, the people of Israel continued operating under a slave mentality. Although God declared them to be a free people, they were still in bondage in their minds because their minds had yet to be renewed.

"Why did we ever leave Egypt?" (Numbers 11:20) *Essentially,* they were asking, *"Why did we ever leave our bondage?"* Believing that their bondage was better than what God had to offer them. Bondage is a place of confinement and that confined place could be a mental place, a spiritual place or a physical place. Although bondage has a

negative connotation, there is an unexplainable sense of comfortability that is found there, especially if you've been in it for years. Although I was living in bondage, I didn't want to be free because I was comfortable just like the Israelites. I enjoyed it because it was a snug place for me, and it was all I have ever known.

The reason why Israel rhetorically asked, *"Why did we ever leave Egypt?"* was because they realized that the place that the Lord wanted to bring them into was a place that pushed them beyond their level of comfortability. God promised them that the land that He was bringing them into was a rich land that flowed with milk and honey (Numbers 14:7) but the journey to the promise wasn't easy so they complained, murmured, whined and regretted ever leaving Egypt because it was a place of comfort to them. Egypt was all the Israelites have ever known.

When you're living in bondage, you don't have to do a lot. All that bondage requires of you is for you to remain. The Israelites complained on their way to their Promise Land because it required more of them. *"Why is the Lord taking us to this country to have us die in battle?" (Numbers 14:3)* they whined. The people of Israel were so used to living a mediocre and mundane life that was spent by building brick and mortar every day but when God called them out of Egypt to possess their possession they were given commands to do something that they weren't used to and that was to act.

"When you cross the Jordan River into the land of Canaan, you must drive out all the people living there. You must destroy their carved and molten images and demolish all their pagan shrines. Take possession of the land and settle in it, because I have given it to you to occupy."* (Numbers 34: 51-53)

In order to receive the promise, they had to pursue the promise. The promise wasn't going to be handed to them, they had to lay hold of what rightfully belonged to them as sons of God. The land of Canaan was their inheritance, always has been and always will be. But obtaining this place required the Israelites to act on faith, belief, boldness, courage and complete and total trust in God's leadership and promises over their lives.

The people of Israel constantly compared where the Lord brought them out of to where the Lord was bringing them into. *"If only the LORD had killed us back in Egypt,"* they moaned. *"There we sat around pots filled with meat and ate all the bread we wanted. But now you have brought us into this wilderness to starve us all to death." (Exodus 10:3)* How crazy do they sound? You were once a slave and now God has called you into sonship. Someone has offered you freedom and there is an opportunity for you to break free from what's been holding you captive your entire life, but you refuse the offer because you desire comfort more than you desire becoming?

I have always been comfortable living in fear. Even after I gave my life to Christ, I was still operating like the Israelites, comparing my life before Christ to the new life that I now had. Afraid to lay hold of what rightfully belonged to me not just as a child, but as a son of God. Fear was so comfortable, and I was always frightened by anything that pushed me beyond the limitations that I had set for myself. It wasn't until I allowed the Lord to begin to transform me into a new person by changing the way that I think (Romans 12: 2). This transformation process didn't take place overnight, but it began with my decision to believe what His word said about me and in His word I found out that *"I was no longer a slave to fear, but that I am a child of God." (Galatians 4:7)*

How many times have you refused to step into all that God has called you to be because you've gotten comfortable with where you currently are? Often, what we fail to realize is that our refusal to become is not only a denial of what God has for you, it's a denial of who you are. When you refuse to take the land and fully step into all that God has called you to become, you're saying that what God has for you isn't enough. God is completely sovereign, and He doesn't need you to do anything, rather, He wants *for* you. He wants you to step into the Promised Land and take possession of everything that rightfully belongs to you as son of God. He wants *for* you to become everything that He has called you to become but we can never fully become unless we choose to leave our bondage, our baggage, our sin, our failures, our mistakes, our insecurities and all of our defense mechanisms in Egypt.

You cannot enter into a new territory, a new state, start a new business venture or enter a courtship with old ways of thinking and old habits. The old you must die in Egypt because where God is taking you mandates for you to be healed, delivered, whole, free and renewed in your way of thinking not only about yourself but also about God.

ENCOUNTERING THE SEEKER

I have spent most of my life hiding but when I gave my life to Jesus Christ in December of 2011 I realized that I could hide from people all I wanted but the one person, the one being that I couldn't hide from was God. I thought I was such a good hider until I realized that God has had his eyes set on me since before, I was even born. Psalm 139 lays it all out so effortlessly for me.

THE RIGHT TO BECOME

*LORD, you have examined my heart
and know everything about me.
² You know when I sit down or stand
up. You know my thoughts even when
I'm far away ³ You see me when I
travel and when I rest at home.
You know everything I do.
⁴ You know what I am going to say
even before I say it, LORD.
⁵ You go before me and follow me.
You place your hand of blessing on
my head. ⁶ Such knowledge is too
wonderful for me,
too great for me to understand !⁷ I
can never escape from your Spirit!
I can never get away from your
presence! ⁸ If I go up to heaven, you
are there, if I go down to the
grave,[a] you are there. ⁹ If I ride the
wings of the morning,
if I dwell by the farthest oceans,
¹⁰ even there your hand will guide me,
and your strength will support me.
¹¹ I could ask the darkness to hide me
and the light around me to become
night— ¹² but even in darkness I
cannot hide from you. To you the
night shines as bright as day.
Darkness and light are the same to
you. ¹³ You made all the delicate, inner
parts of my body
and knit me together in my mother's
womb.¹⁴ Thank you for making me so
wonderfully complex! Your
workmanship is marvelous—how well
I know it. ¹⁵ You watched me as I was
being formed in utter seclusion,
as I was woven together in the dark
of the womb. ¹⁶ You saw me before I
was born. Every day of my life was
recorded in your book.
Every moment was laid out
before a single day had passed.
¹⁷ How precious are your thoughts
about me,[b] O God.
They cannot be numbered!
¹⁸ I can't even count them;
they outnumber the grains of sand!
And when I wake up,
you are still with me!"*

The first time I read this passage, it was like trying to swallow a huge capsule size pill. I just couldn't get it down. There was no amount of saliva and water that my mouth had that allowed me to swallow the mega truths of Psalm 139. My wounded and fractured heart couldn't

2

take the fact the God of the universe *sees* me. And not only does He see me, but He also *knows* me. He knows every. single. thing. about. me. This aggravated me. My heart raged when I found this out because I have tried everything in my life to keep from being seen and known only to come to find out that the truth of the matter is that before I was even in my mother's womb God *knew* me.

Taking in these truths have been the hardest thing for me to do. Accepting the fact that I am known has been the bane of my entire existence and I know that that may sound slightly dramatic, but it's my reality. This entire time, the delicate intricate details of my life have been *known* and *seen*. I cannot begin to tell you how uncomfortable this made me feel (and still does if I'm completely honest). I realized that it didn't matter how much I tried; I couldn't hide from God. It didn't matter where I was, whether it's at home or on campus, at my retail job or in my basement. *God sees me.* He sees right through me. His eyes saw my unformed body when I was in my mother's womb. He saw my ligaments, tendons, bone marrows, joints, blood vessels all while they were still being formed. God *saw* me. I wasn't even a complete human-being yet, but His eyes still saw me. Coming to terms with this has gripped my heart like none other. There was a tug-of-war, a true WrestleMania match going on in my heart between God and my fears. Every day I was faced with the question of: *Should I let go of what I've been holding onto all these years or should I try something new, something that I've never done before and cling onto someone else for a change?*

I have spent all my life living in a shell of obscurity and If I'm being honest with you, I didn't want to break free from it because that shell was my safe haven. I knew that the moment that I broke free from that shell it meant that I had to rely on someone else for safety and I wasn't sure if I was ready for that. There was a source of satisfaction and comfort that I found in that shell. The shell was warm and cozy, and it offered me the thing that I desired the most: protection.

You are known by God. You are known by God. You are known my God. You, Joycelyn Ogunsola are known by God. This is what the whole of Psalm 139 kept emphasizing to me. All I wanted to do was scream, "NOOOO! I DON'T WANT TO BE KNOWN BY YOU!" I rejected it. I refused it. I denied it. I pushed it away. I didn't want it. I was safe where I was. But those words kept ringing in my mind and insinuating to me that it was too late. The Creator of the universe *knows* me. His fiery eyes are constantly gazing upon my very being day and night, night and day because He doesn't sleep nor slumber.

Everything in me wanted to surrender but fear told me to hold onto its grip. Psalm 139: 11-12 says, *"I could ask the darkness to hide me, and the light around me to become night—but even in darkness I cannot hide from you. To you the night shines as bright as day. Darkness and light are the same to you."* Even when I'm in the darkest moments of despair, I still can't hide from Him. God sees me just as clearly in the dark as He does in the light. I realized that it wasn't that I couldn't hide from him, it was the fact that I was never hidden from Him to begin with. God saw my past; He sees my present and He sees my future. I couldn't get over that.

A part of me really thought I was a good hider but come to find out, God has scoped out every single one of my hiding places and He knows everything there is to know about me and this made me feel so vulnerable. So even when I try to hide, I can't because I'm already seen. He already sees me and all I am left to do is give in and completely surrender to the truth, the truth that says that I am *known* by God.

So, to all my hiders out there, know this: God sees you. Even in the tightest of hiding places, He sees you. There's absolutely nothing that you do that catches Him by surprise or throws Him of course. The whole plot twist of the "Hide-And-Go-Seek" game was that it didn't matter where I hid; I was bound to be found, pursued, known, loved and sought after by a God who has always known my end from my beginning.

THE RIGHT TO BECOME

2

The Beginning of A Lie

I remember being a little girl and how every time my mom would leave for work; I would always go to my parent's room and fish through her closet for clothes to try on. I loved playing dress up. I would walk around the house in her clothes that were two times my size and in her shoes that were 6 sizes too big. Upstairs, where all the bedrooms were located there was a corridor and I saw that space as my runway. I would walk down that short hallway and strut in my mother's clothes and "present" myself to my father. This was my way of asking... *"Daddy am I lovely? Am I beautiful?"* He would always clap his hands in approval and say *"Great!", "Awesome!"* and *"You are wonderful!"* and I took all of those things to heart, but it wasn't what my young feminine heart needed to hear. What I simply needed to hear was... *"You are beautiful."* But I never did.

However, I do distinctly remember my mom calling me beautiful maybe once or twice but around the age that she began to voice it, it was a little too late because another voice had crept in and completely infiltrated my psyche.

MUSIC CLASS BLUES

In 8th grade, Mr. Brown's music class was the class that I always looked forward to. I remember memories of him always greeting the class with warm melodies. The atmosphere that he created in the classroom was one that was always inviting, and his authentic personality allotted everyone the freedom to express themselves through music. It didn't matter to him if you were musically inclined or not, he made sure that everyone was engaged in some way during class and we were.

The class was mixed with various ethnic groups but whenever we would sing a chorus, Mr. Brown had a way of making us feel like we were all one. In middle school, the people that were mixed were the ones that usually had a reputation for being the most attractive people in the school and the one ethnicity that everyone raved over was Afro-Asians or "Blasians" as we would call them. "Blasians" had a very high reputation for being known as attractive and exotic looking people and we had one of those in Mr. Brown's class. Her name was Jasmine, and Jasmine knew that she was pretty. Not only did she know that she was pretty, but everyone in her class knew as well.

One day, during class, Jasmine came over to where I was sitting, sat down in front of me, looked me straight in my eyes and said..."*You ugly.*" And as she sat there, she continued to stare me down, waiting to see if I was going to respond. But I didn't. I mean, I couldn't because I had nothing to counteract what she said. So, I sat there and believed it. That was the beginning of the lie that I went on to believing for several years.

Whenever the question of your identity is left unanswered, the enemy will use it as an opportunity to plant seeds of deception. This is exactly what he did in that moment. A seed was sown that day that became the root of most (if not all) of the insecurities that I dealt with throughout my teenage years and a little into my adulthood. Jasmine was the first voice that told me who I was. I have not the fondest memory of any other voice prior to hers. Because she was the first voice, I believed what she said and accepted it as my truth. From that day on I believed that I was ugly.

What's interesting is that in 6th grade I was this bubbly, fun-loving, personable little girl. I was very open, vibrant and alive and no one could tell me anything. Things were going well for the 11-year-old Joycelyn but then 6th grade ended, and I had to transition into middle school. 7th grade was all a blur for me. 8th grade came around and that was when the enemy's program for my life kicked in. That one little lie shut the vibrancy of my entire life down. From that day forward I went into an internal cave and I hid from the world. Why?

Because I thought I was hideous. I thought that I was repulsive, that I couldn't show my face and that I had no real beauty to offer the world.

After this instance happened, I got promoted from middle school to high school and in high school I suffered with an extreme amount of depression and I was known as the sad girl. Sad and *ugly*? What a combination.

Beauty and I had no form of association. It didn't matter what piece of clothing that I wore or the amount of make-up that I put on my face, I still believed that I was ugly and no matter how much I tried, I felt like I just couldn't be beautiful. That was the reality that I lived in. Ugly was who I was.

Ugly is something that is unpleasant or repulsive in nature and ugly things don't deserve to be given attention. When something is ugly, people usually look away because it's unpleasant and dissatisfying. And because Jasmine said I was ugly, I believed that I was unpleasant and dissatisfying. I believed that whenever someone looked at me, they were utterly repulsed by my sight and this caused me to withdraw myself from people. I limited my interactions with both men and women to keep them from seeing how ugly I was. If an interaction with someone was mandatory, I made sure to always maintain minimal eye-contact with that person. I constantly walked with my head down and struggled with looking people in the eyes. I kept to myself because I assumed that if Jasmine thought that I was ugly, then surely everyone else must think the same about me. I envied the girls that were confident and knew that they were beautiful. I wanted to be free to be myself, but I didn't even know who I truly was.

In a world that was created by Beauty and filled with beauty, I felt like an outcast. I felt like I didn't belong. If women were created to reflect the beauty of God in this world in a way that no other created thing can and if I, being a young girl, believed that I wasn't beautiful then why was I living? What could I possibly offer the world?

If you're a man reading this, please do not skip over this section of reading. The situation that happened to me in Mr. Brown's music class has happened to many young girls and women all around the world and it cuts deeper than you may (or may not) be thinking. Many women have believed lies that said they were ugly, unattractive, unappealing, not good enough and that they simply just have no true beauty to offer the world. But as I stated earlier, whenever the question of your identity is left unanswered the enemy will use that as an opportunity to plant seeds of deception.

There are so many women who have been lied to and have been living their lives centered around those very lies. I believe all women across the world can attest to the fact that we all want to be told that we are beautiful and when we are not told this it affects us tremendously. It affects our confidence and self-esteem; it causes us to compare ourselves to other women and sometimes even envy other women for their own unique beauty. It doesn't matter how many times a woman is told that she is beautiful, if she doesn't believe it for herself first, then it will never take root in her heart.

God created women to be beautiful and when a woman believes that she is anything other than what God created her to be it's an attack on her femininity. In the same manner, when a man believes that he is anything other than what God created him to be, it serves as an attack on his masculinity. S God never dumbs down the physical beauty of a woman, but He constantly affirms it. So, men, I implore you, as husbands, fathers and leaders, please endeavor to seek and understand the importance of beauty as it pertains to women. Beauty is not everything and yes, it is fleeting but it's still important and it's important to the women that are in your life.

What I experienced in 8th grade was an attack on my femininity. Those two words bruised my heart in a way that I was never able to unpack until just recently. I grew up looking at other women on the T.V, in magazines and even in the grocery store wishing and secretly questioning why God didn't make me *"pretty like her"*. I even felt ashamed of my innate desire of wanting to be beautiful not realizing that my desire to be beautiful wasn't a shameful thing. In fact, it was a good desire that came from God. Not only did God create me to beautiful, He wants me to be beautiful, to look beautiful and to feel beautiful.

I didn't know it then but as I was beginning to mature into womanhood, I realized that the deep desires of our hearts are key indicators to that which you were created for. If you have a desire to be a mother or a father, a husband or a wife, then you were created to be those things. God placed that desire in you for a reason. If you have a desire to be loved, you were created to be loved by Love Himself. If you have a desire to be beautiful, then my darling you were created to be just that. I longed to be beautiful. It was always a deep desire of my heart that I've always felt ashamed of not realizing that the very thing that I was ashamed to be was the very reason why God created me, and it was who I already was.

It has taken years to uproot one lie that I've believed for so long. I've been believing this lie longer than I've been believing the truth so when I first encountered the truth of God's word that said I was fearfully and wonderfully made, that I was altogether beautiful and that there was no flaw in me, it was so hard for me to believe. Although I was reading it and declaring it over my life it seemed like God's word was impenetrable. This seed that was planted by the enemy through a young girl had taken so much root in heart to the point where it affected every single area of my life and it left no room for me to believe anything else.

Years passed after I gave my life to Christ my mindset regarding my beauty was still the same. I shared with different people in passing about this deeply rooted lie that affected me in every area of my life and they always pointed me back to the scriptures. But I still believed that I was ugly. I still believed that I had no beauty to offer the world. So, I started to believe that maybe God's word wasn't as infallible as many have claimed it to be. Maybe it was all fluff and it was all too good to be true. Maybe Jasmine was right. Maybe I was ugly. Maybe this was the only truth that I was destined to believe for the rest of my life.

Once a lie has been planted, it can take years for it to be uprooted. I was always ashamed to say that even after being saved for almost 8 years, I still find it hard to believe in God's word over my life. I still have my days where I do doubt the supremacy of His word but I'm learning that I have the right to be beautiful because God made me this way. I am not the same insecure little girl that I was in 8th grade. I have grown in confidence tremendously over the past couple of years and every day I am still learning, growing and rightfully becoming who He has called me to become. It has taken constant repetition of the word of God, pulling down strongholds, thoughts and any high and lofty thing that wants me to believe anything other than who my God says I am. Indeed, I am everything that God says that I am. Fearfully, wonderfully and beautifully made.

THE RIGHT TO BECOME

3

My Biggest Failure

I graduated from high school in the Spring of 2014 and unlike most of my peers, I didn't know what I wanted to do with my life. Growing up, I thought that I wanted to become a pediatrician but after I got saved in December of 2011, I quickly realized that medicine was not the avenue that I wanted to pursue in life. While coming to terms with this reality, I still struggled with figuring out what I wanted to major in and me questioning my major led to the ultimate question of what my life's purpose was.

THE RIGHT TO BECOME

I started college in the Fall of 2014 completely undecided not only about what to major in but about where I wanted to go in life. This uncertainty led me to what I call my "breaking point semester". When I entered college, my first semester was great. I lived on campus, was in a scholarly program and my grades were amazing. I ended the semester off with a banging 3.8 GPA. Although I was glad to have finished off my first semester of college amazingly, I still felt unfulfilled. When I looked to my left and to my right, it felt like everyone around me had a sense of purpose, had already declared a major and knew where they were going in life. I, on the other hand felt aimless and purposeless and on top of that I was still major-less so I did what I knew how to do, I prayed.

Spring 2015 was when I finally decided that I was not going to live a purposeless life anymore. I needed to know why on earth I was created. Reading the book, "Purpose Driven Life" by Rick Warren wasn't enough for me. I needed to hear from the Creator Himself why He placed me on this earth. For the entire semester, I found myself slowly withdrawing away from my academics in pursuit of purpose. To me, it was far bigger than declaring a major, I desperately needed to know what the meaning behind my existence was, so I sought the face of God like my life depended on it.

School slowly but surely became disinteresting to me. 11:59 p.m. no longer mattered and the times when I was supposed to be in class, I spent in my dorm room crying out to God for Him to reveal to me who I was and who He created me to be.

Time progressed and God slowly but surely began to reveal the significance behind my life. One day, while sitting in my parent's living room I uttered six words that wouldn't make sense to anyone at the time. *"I'm going to write a book,"* was what I said. No one was around me. It was just me and my thoughts. So, I spoke those words again but this time with a little more confidence believing that the book was already written. *"I'm going to write a book!"* Mind you, I was an 18-year-old freshman in college, with no job, no money and I had no knowledge about book-writing or self-publishing. All I had was an idea and I carried that idea with me until I saw what I spoke become a living reality in my life. At this point, I still wasn't clear on what my purpose was but I had six words that I wholeheartedly believed were given to me by the Holy Spirit and at the time God knew that it was just enough for me to jumpstart my life.

Why tell an 18-year-old college freshman to write a book? It was completely ludacris! Of course, everyone talked me out of it. *"Um, writing a book is expensive Joycelyn"*, a friend of mine said. *"A book? Huh?! That's pretty random don't you think?"* another friend suggested. Then of course my loving parents said, *"Finish school first then you can write a book."* I heard it all, but I wasn't going to allow anyone to stop my determination. I heard a word from the Lord, and I took off running with it...literally!

Instantly, I began doing research on how to write a book. Everything from the estimated cost of publishing to the difference between traditional and self-publishing, to editing, typesetting, getting a book cover design, purchasing an ISBN number, getting the book copyrighted and purchasing an LLC. I even invested in taking workshops and webinars to enhance my knowledge about self-publishing. At eighteen, I had no idea that what I was doing was going to turn into a business. I wasn't even pursuing it for the money, I pursued it because I believed that it was what the Lord wanted me to do. I wasn't after the money or any of the attention that would come from it, I was after my purpose.

Purpose was my driving force and I took off with instant speed and didn't allow any other driver to cut me off on the road to getting this book published. But all the while, in pursuit of writing my first book, titled "Revealing of the Sons of God", as I stated earlier, I put my academics on the back burner. My eagerness for purpose so consumed me to the point where I didn't even care about school anymore. During the time of me writing my book, I was involved in a campus ministry called, Bethel Campus Fellowship serving as Vice-President, Secretary and Sisters Fellowship Coordinator all during different semesters of my undergrad career. My e-board members and people within the ministry all knew that I was endeavoring to publish a book, but no one knew that I was struggling in school. It wasn't that I didn't want to tell anyone, it was more so that I didn't care enough to tell anyone. I finally had a glimpse of what my purpose was, and I was so blinded by my efforts that I completely neglected my academics.

After Spring 2015, semester after semester passed and I would find myself either failing a class, having to withdraw from a class (because I didn't want to fail) or getting either a "C" or a "D" in a class. Because of this, my GPA went from a 3.8 to a 1.9. I received a letter from the university that I was attending warning me that because my GPA had reached under a 2.0 I was on academic probation and that if I didn't make efforts to raise it, I would be academically dismissed from the school. Completely ignoring the warning signs that God gave me, I moved on with my life and I continued in pursuing my book writing endeavors.

The semester of Spring 2017 came around and I ended up releasing my book on January 26th, 2017. I took about 5 classes this semester and I found myself ending up failing two more classes and obtaining C's and D's in the other classes that I was taking. At the end of the semester I took a good look at my transcripts and I finally came to my senses and realized that I needed to get my whole academic life together. I made efforts to take summer classes to retake the classes that I failed but by the time I was ready to finally pick up my slack it was already too late.

Summer 2017 I received a letter from Bowie State University informing me that my GPA fell below a 2.0 for two academic semesters in a row and that because of this, I was unable to return to the university for a whole academic year. When I read this letter, it was like everything in my world stopped. I couldn't believe it. *"Joycelyn, how did you get here?!"* was what I kept asking myself as tears streamed down my face. I simply could not believe it. It was in this moment that I believed that I had ruined my life.

Through my tears, I was prompted by the Holy Spirit to grab one of my old journals and I stumbled upon old entries that I wrote during my whole book writing process. One entry wrote, *"Joycelyn, just because I told you to write a book doesn't mean that you should neglect your academics."* and *"School is still important, make sure you complete your homework."* The Lord speaks to me a lot through writing and these warning signs were clear as day, but I never took heed. The Lord was speaking but I wasn't listening.

After I received this devastating news, I didn't tell anyone for about a week because of the amount of shame that I was bearing. But I realized that I couldn't keep this a secret forever so the first set of people that I opened up to were my (then) mentors. They encouraged me and gave me hope but the amount of pain, shame, guilt and condemnation that I felt had already clogged up my ears. There was nothing that they said that could change the fact that I felt like my entire life was over.

The Summer of 2017 was the worst summer of my life. I was battling depression, anxiety, shame, failure and defeat. Every day I was being tormented in my sleep and I woke up with the weight of shame pounding in my chest. For about nine to ten months I decided to cut off all social interactions with people, even my closest friends. I deactivated all of my social media accounts. I isolated myself from my community and stopped going to fellowship outings. If there was a birthday dinner, a cookout, a worship night or a conference I made sure that I made no reservations to attend. It even got to a point where I wanted to take my newly published book off all distribution sites.

Shortly after the book was published, I had a book signing event and I remembered that I still had some hard copies left over from the event just sitting in my closet. One day through intense tears, I grabbed one of the hard copies of the books and aggressively started tearing the pages up. I was furious because of all the chaos and confusion that was happening in my life began when I started writing this book. I thought maybe I should have just listened to those who wanted to talk me out of it and allow them to talk me out of it. I felt like a complete and total failure.

"Joycelyn, how did you get here?" was the question that I kept asking myself that summer. Me failing out of school crushed me mentally, emotionally, spiritually and physically. I felt like a bowling pin that had been knocked down and I didn't know how to get back up. It was too dark for me to see the light at the end of the tunnel. My life became stagnant and motionless. I lost my joy, my peace and my sense of purpose. Even my relationship with God was on the edge of the fence. Although His word says that we have access to approach His throne of grace boldly I felt too ashamed to even do so.

Even though I knew that me failing out of school didn't serve as a surprise to God, relating to Him became a huge struggle for me because I felt unworthy and condemned. How could I stand before a faultless and spotless God with all my guilt, shame and failure? I felt unworthy of His presence. I felt unworthy of beholding His beauty completing forgetting that it is in me beholding His beauty that I forget about the ugliness of what I did and that I am forever changed.

It wasn't until after I published the book that I realized that the sole reason as to why the Lord had me write *"Revealing of the Sons of God"* was so that I could get healed, set free and delivered. Me publishing my first book was God's way of breaking my shell, cracking my cocoon and bursting the bubble that I've lived in for so long. God used me writing a book as a tool for me to come out of hiding and the enemy knew that. The whole message behind the book was identity. From the first page to the final page, the book spoke solely on identity and the importance of knowing who you are as a son of God.

Throughout the book writing process, the Lord took His time in revealing to me who I was. He stripped away every sense of self that I had and wanted to make sure that I was fully convinced in my heart that I was everything that He said I was according to His Word. Me releasing the book broke me free. I came out of hiding and the Lord was able to do what He had always wanted to do, which was to reveal and announce me to the world.

After the book release, when I tell you that the enemy waged war, he did. He threw a giant fit and he used my failure to the best of his advantage. The enemy attacked who God proclaimed that I was. It wasn't long until after receiving that letter that I began to believe the lies of the enemy all over again. It was like everything that the Lord taught me about identity, sonship, purpose and His love were completely thrown out the window by this one act of failure. It was like the enemy knew that the shame that would come from failing out of school would be strong enough to cause me to go right back to the place that God once delivered me out from and guess what? It did.

Completely unaware of the enemy's schemes and tactics and living in a state of oblivion, the very thing that the Lord delivered me from, I found myself back in. I felt like Jonathan McReynolds song "Cycles" completely exemplified this season of my life. I was going in cycles and I didn't know how to break free from it. I thought I had lost the very little credibility that I had as a young self-published Author and so I did the very thing that I knew how to do best, I hid.

As I stated in chapter 1, hiding was always my thing. I was good at it and this failure presented the perfect opportunity for me to do so. As the months transpired, I found myself safe and secure in this hiding place. I was comfortable and I was right where the enemy wanted me to be. Hidden, afraid, insecure, ashamed, guilty and condemned. The devil had me wrapped around his fingers and I fell right into the pit that he dug for me. The weight of shame that I was carrying was so heavy to the point where it began manifesting itself in the physical and I started gaining weight. I was so stressed to the point where I started to break out in places that I've never broken out before. The weight gain and the acne breakouts gave me valid points to hide. I did not want to be seen 10 pounds heavier than I was with breakouts all over my face, so I continued masking my shame, pain and disgrace in a cave.

THE RIGHT TO BECOME

It took me the whole the whole summer to muster up enough strength and courage to tell my family. I was experiencing the biggest internal war that I have ever faced. As the summer days went by, the upcoming semester would be approaching and every day I was faced with the painful thought of knowing that I had to tell my family this news that I knew would break their hearts.

I received the letter in June, but I didn't end up telling my parents until August. It was precisely the week before the semester started. I wanted to hold out for as much as I could because I greatly feared what their response would be. *What would they do? What would they say?* I wanted to sit my entire family down and tell them the news all in one sitting, but I ended up telling all of them individually. I started with my siblings then worked my way to my parents.

The day that I broke the news to my dad, I took him to the library and told him my whole academic journey from beginning to end. I explained all the ins and outs and ups and downs to him. He listened and internalized everything that I said before he gave me a response. After I was done talking, he asked," Are *you done talking?"* I responded, *"Yes."* and he says, *"Okay, let's go."* We walk to the car and in the car is when he gives me his response. I took a deep breath and he begins to talk. *"This is a huge disappointment but you're still my child, I can't throw you away. And I don't look at this as failure. Failure to me is when you give up, so what's your plan for the next school year?"* As he's talking tears just started streaming down my face. I was silent. I couldn't talk. All I could do was cry and think "What manner of love is this?" It was in that moment where I was able to experience the tangible love of the Father towards me. My earthly father was affirming my identity, but what he didn't know was that God was using him to reaffirm my sonship.

Failing out of college is probably one of the most shameful and humiliating things that could happen to a Nigerian parent and to see my dad extend so much grace towards me really allowed me to see both my earthly father and my heavenly father in a new way. I was reminded of Romans 8:38 that says, *"And I am convinced that nothing can ever separate us from God's love. Neither death nor life, neither angels nor demons, neither our fears for today nor our worries about tomorrow—not even the powers of hell can separate us from God's love."* I was reminded that there was nothing that I could do that could separate me from God's love...not even my failure. The conversation that I had with my dad in the car that day was one that I will never forget. It opened the door for me to have open communication with my heavenly Father again. It showed me that God still loved me despite my mistakes and that I could still become something.

My dad asking me what my plans were for the whole year that I wasn't in school ignited hope inside of me again. It made me realize that I didn't have to stay where I was and that I still had the potential to rise above my circumstances. Despite me failing out of school, the right to become was still mine. On the cross of Calvary over 2000 years ago, Jesus nailed all my failures, sins, mistakes, shame and guilt (past, present and future) on the cross. He died so that I could become something so that meant that failure wasn't the final verdict over my life. The only thing that was final in my life was the word of God and the word of God says there is no condemnation for those who are in Christ Jesus. So, this meant that I didn't have to continue living in condemnation when I stand forgiven in the sight of my Lord.

After I had a conversation with my dad we went home, and I went to sleep. I woke up the following morning knowing that I had to tell my mom. My parents are complete opposites. My dad is more reserved quiet and rational and my mother on the other hand is more expressive in her tone and speech. I came home from an orientation from work (apart of my plan was to work full-time during me not being in school) and my mom was the one that actually initiated the conversation about school and it was at that point that I knew that I had to tell her everything. I began telling her the story from beginning to end (just like how I told my dad) but I didn't even finish half of the story until she interjected and said, *"So you failed out of school?!".* *"Mommy let me finish telling you the full story. You deserve to know the full story"* was my response but she continued interjecting and demanded an answer from me. So, I said, *"Yes, I failed out of school."*

The moment I answered her was the beginning of a huge uproar. My mom started screaming, cursing, yelling and crying. Her rage was a mix of emotions coupled with anger, confusion, pain, disappointment and frustration. I understood my mom's pain, but her words were so sharp that they pierced my heart. All I could do was just sit there, glued to my seat with tears streaming down my face and a bleeding heart.

"Indeed, you are a failure", "To hell with you!" along with many other curses that left her mouth that I won't repeat just out of respect for my mother, came spewing out her mouth like fire. I accepted it. I believed it. She was right. I was a failure. I was weeping like a baby who was in desperate need of her mother's milk. In that moment, I felt like a little girl who needed a huge embrace from her heavenly father. I needed His embrace and His strength because I felt so downtrodden

and weak. I needed God to tell me that everything was going to be okay and that this too shall pass.

My sister ended up dragging me upstairs to my room where she gave me headphones to listen to worship music to drain out my mother's voice who was still going at it. In my bed, through a snotty nose and tear-filled eyes, I conjured up strength to ask the Lord to first, forgive my mother for the hurting words that she had spoken against me and for me to also forgive her. That night, things eventually died down and I remained in my room for the rest of the night.

The next morning, my mother called my siblings and I into the living room to have a family meeting. Her demeanor was completely different from that of the previous night. She seemed more cool, calm and collected. To my surprise, she opened the family meeting with prayer and started off by saying, *"You see what just happened with Olamide (my middle name) yesterday? Let this serve as an example to you all for it to never happen again."* She then turns to me and says, *"And all those things that I said yesterday, I take them back. You are not a failure. You will graduate. You will succeed. You will rise above your contemporaries. You will forever be the head and not the tail. Always above and never beneath."* I was completely stunned. 14 hours ago, this woman was cursing me and hurling all types of insults into my life and in less than 24 hours, with the same mouth that she used to curse me, she turns around and blesses me. This was the pure work of the Holy Spirit Himself. Only He has the power to convict and change the hearts of man. It didn't make sense to me.

You may have never had an experience where someone, whether it be your mother or father, sister or brother, husband or wife cursed you and then comes back around, repents and starts speaking blessings over you but I'm here to tell you that even if my mother never repented and the Holy Spirit never turned her heart towards me, her words still weren't final. You may have been spoken ill against, ridiculed, judged, condemned and cursed by someone but no one has the power to speak into your life unless you accept it. God is the only one who has legal rights and authority to pronounce and announce who you are. When God says that you are someone then no one can speak against it. When my mom was blessing me, it wasn't her that was speaking, it was the Lord. He was speaking through her and reminding me of who I was in Him. He reminded me that I was justified, redeemed, renewed and restored in Him.

I'm so glad that I ended up not telling my parents at the same time because I wouldn't have been able to reap the benefits that came from both of their responses. From my father's response I learned that failure wasn't strong enough to separate me from my Heavenly Father's love towards me. Although I failed, I was still a child of God, I was still a son and I still had a rich and glorious inheritance in Christ Jesus. Nothing changed. From my mother's response, I learned that God is a redeemer. I was able to see how he was able to redeem my confidence, my identity and my sonship.

OLD JOURNAL ENTRY

God, I can't function properly without you. How am I supposed to even show my face? What will people say? What will people think when they hear that I failed out of school? Am I crazy? Is something wrong with me? Did I really learn my lesson or was it just all a mask? I'm so tempted to go into hiding again. I'm so tempted to delete my Instagram and go into a cave and just live there. But part of me knows that this is exactly what the enemy wants. He wants me to live in a cave where there is no light, no freedom, no sunshine, no rain...just darkness, sadness and gloomy days. He wants my freedom, he wants my happiness, he wants my joy. After-all, he only came to steal, kill and destroy.

God I am so imperfect and I'm like the least of these. Why can't my life be perfect? Why couldn't I just go to college and graduate after 4 years like most people and obtain a degree? Why couldn't I just focus in school? Why did I have to write the book? I would be well further along in life than I am now. I would have a degree. My parents would be so proud of me. They wouldn't have to worry. They wouldn't have to be afraid of my future. Everything would be okay. I would be okay.

I brought so much shame and disgrace on my family and even myself. Have I truly forgiven myself? Have I truly let go of my mistakes?

How can God use this? How can He use me? The very thing that He has called me to do, I fall short of it daily. How? What is wrong with me? Do I need deliverance? What needs to be broken off me? What will my friends say/think of me?

I think I was so afraid to make the same mistake again that I didn't even try this time around. But the crazy thing about it is that you foreknew all of this. God, you knew me even before I was in my mother's womb and you knew how every single day would look like long before it came to pass. You knew. You knew that I would fail out of school. You knew that I would focus more on the book than my academics. You knew it all and despite all that I've done, you still have a beautiful plan for my life. Although, I don't see the big picture, you do so give me grace to trust your sovereign plan for my life. Please...Lord, give me grace.

I was insecure whenever people brought up school because I knew I wasn't doing well, and I never wanted to talk about. But I knew that what you don't reveal, you can't heal.

GOD'S RESPONSE: No one is going to understand. No one is going to get it. But they won't say anything about you because I have you covered. I am your defender. I am your defense. I have you protected. Remember what I told you? Your life is not going to look like anything this world has ever seen. Do not compare your life to another person's life. It's going to look exactly the way that I want it to look. I understand. I get you and your feelings and thoughts are valid. Isaiah 40:28 says, "Have you not seen? Have you never understood? I am the everlasting God, the Creator of all of the earth. I never grow weak or weary. No one can measure the depths of my understanding." Your pain is valid. Your disappointment is valid. But you don't have to use the validity of my pain to try to apprehend the depths of it. Understand that I will be my defender. I oversee your reputation but if you continue defending and protecting yourself then you leave me no room to do that for you. Part of your healing requires that you come out of hiding and stand boldly in my marvelous light... so come out of hiding my love... it's time to come and allow yourself to be seen again.

JOYCELYN OGUNSOLA

THE RIGHT TO BECOME

4

Becoming God's Woman

Senior year of high school was the worst for me. Now, I know you're probably thinking what could a 17- year-old possibly be struggling with other than filling out her FAFSA for the first time? But trust me when I tell you, I wasn't just any 17-year-old girl. I was a 17-year-old girl who at the time was walking with the Lord for two years with no spiritual guidance. I was figuring out how to put God first, how to deal with all my internal struggles, my family struggles, and not to mention past issues that had now resurfaced.

As much as I loved God, I was young, I was naïve, I was struggling, and I was looking for a way out. I was looking for something that was better than the current life that I was living. I needed a savior and at the time I was looking to college to be my sweet saving grace, because let's be honest... I had Jesus, or at least I thought I did. Who knows? I was too weary to discern His voice at the time. But I needed something more. Something that looked appealing and it was Spelman.

I really believed that me going to Spelman would make all the difference in my life, that it would be my escape route because if I'm completely honest, senior year of high-school was one of the worst years of my life-spiritually, academically and relationally. You name it and I was going through it. All in all, I still had hope and I saw myself for what I could become. I thought that going to college would really solve all my problems. I would be away from my mom and all our constant back and forth arguments, I would be away from all my family struggles and going to Spelman was my escape route.

MY DREAM WOMAN, MY DREAM SCHOOL

I remember how the process of applying for college was both exciting and nerve-wracking. Exciting, because I already knew that I wanted to attend none other than the illustrious Spelman College. Nerve-wrecking, because, well I was applying for college. I had a lot of mixed emotions during this season of my life but one thing that I was sure of was that Spelman embodied everything that I was looking for in an institution of higher learning. Aside from receiving an education that would ultimately propel me for my future there were many other things I had to consider when choosing a college. I mean everything from the cost, to the accreditation of the school, the geographical location, the population size, the cost, the demographics, the school statistics, the cost, the majors/program studies they provide and oh did I mention *the cost*?!

Although I knew that these factors (along with many others) played a huge role in my decision making; there was one other factor that I held in high regard. I was looking to attend far more than just a school that would give me a chance at obtaining a degree. I was looking to attend a college that would propel me to become the woman that I wanted to become. I wanted to go somewhere that would give me experiences, opportunities to develop and a chance to really grow and mature into womanhood. And for me, Spelman College was that school.

Everything that Spelman represented as a college was everything that I wanted for myself as a woman. The excellence, strength, leadership, confidence, courage, grit, determination and passion that I wanted, I looked to Spelman to be the giver of these qualities. Spelman was a school that I believed would inspire me to be the change that I wanted to see in this world as a woman. I fell in love with this school because I could envision myself walking through the campus, walking the halls, taking the classes and just embracing my femininity. There was just something about becoming a Spelmanite woman that intrigued me.

Because I had a strong desire to attend this prominent school, I began to pray and ask God if ultimately this was His will for my life. Then one evening while I was reading my Bible, I heard Him speak, in the clearest voice I have ever heard, saying, *"You're going to Spelman."*

and of course I was ecstatic! I thought, surely the Lord does grant unto His children the desires of their hearts. So, I took this as confirmation and with total faith, I confidently applied to Spelman College even though I didn't meet all their necessary academic requirements. Regardless, I still believed that this was the school that I was going to attend not only because I had an earnest desire to attend but because I believed that I had God's backing on this.

A couple of months went by and we were now nearing Thanksgiving break and the first letter that came in from Spelman College was in a big envelope that basically said that I got wait-listed. I remember telling my father this semi-sad news and asking him to pray that God would just touch the hearts of the people who work in the admissions office (because clearly, they didn't get the memo that God told me I was going to Spelman). About a month or so later, the final letter came, and this time it wasn't in a big powder-blue envelope, it was in a regular 4 ½ by 9 envelope, you know the type of envelopes that you get from your bank just informing you about the transactions that you made from the last two months, yeah that's what I got. But before I even opened the letter, I already knew what it was.

A rejection letter.

When I read the letter, surprisingly, I didn't cry. Rather, the thoughts in my head were somewhere along the lines of... *"Okay God so if I'm not going to Spelman then where am I going?"* If Spelman wasn't in the picture, then what school is? I had only applied to a couple other schools in Maryland and the only options were University of Maryland Eastern Shore or my local community college. I for one knew that I was not going to spend my first year of college at home, so community college was way out of the question for me. One day, I had a conversation with one of my friend's older sister's and we discussed what my plans were, and she mentioned Bowie State University. The following day, I took a visit to the school, applied and received onsite admission. I put down a rooming deposit and in August and within two weeks I moved into Bowie State University.

It's crazy how things don't work out according to our own plans and purposes but according to His. But you know what's even crazier is that I still remember the day that God spoke to me in (what I thought was) the clearest voice ever saying, *"You're going to Spelman."* I sat down and thought to myself, *"God, did I hear you wrong? Was I too quick to jump? Did I not take enough time to listen and hear your voice?"* Now looking back 5 years later, in retrospect, I realized that I didn't take the time out to consult with God about me attending Spelman. I never asked Him what He thought about the school or if He even thought it was a good fit for me. I had already made up my mind that I was going to Spelman and I wasn't going to allow any other voice to manipulate my decision (not even God's).

How many times have you manipulated the voice of God in your life? We can easily mistake what we want to believe or hear for "hearing God's voice" especially when we don't have the willingness to approach Him concerning specific areas in our lives. When we come to

God with our minds already made up about a situation or circumstance, we don't leave room for the Father to speak so we take what we already settled in our minds as "the voice of God", run with it and say, *"God said...",* when in all actuality He didn't even say anything. You didn't even allow Him to speak. That was all you. Then we get upset at God and begin to question if we're even hearing correctly and say, *"But God, I thought you said..."* and that's exactly what I did.

I had my mind made up and settled on attending Spelman and I didn't want to be open about anything else. I really believed that I was going to Spelman so when I received the rejection letter, I found myself right back at the feet of Jesus. I thought it was amazing because in His infinite mercy, He still uses even our mistakes to draw us to Himself and show us that it was His voice that we needed to hear this whole time.

I realized that I had been putting all my hope, confidence, security and sense of fulfillment into an institution rather than putting all of this in God. I was trusting and believing that Spelman would make me and mold me into the woman that *I thought* I wanted to become rather than trusting God to be the Maker of my life. I had forgotten that He was the one who knew me before I was even in my mother's womb. He was the one who created me.

He was the one that was behind my conceptualization. He was the one that recorded every single one of days in His book. He chose my gender. He wanted me here and He wanted me female. So if I wanted to grow and become this woman that He foreknew before the foundations of the world then I needed to look to Him; not to an institution, an organization, a magazine, social media or any other ideology that the world pressures women to look to. I had to look to the one who formed and fashioned me in a place of utter seclusion. I had to look to the God who knows me and sees me.

I had to trust that the same God who created both male and female in His image and likeness would be the same God who would grow me into womanhood. I needed to be reminded of I had forgotten that I was created for His pleasure. I had forgotten that my life is not my own and I saw how this school that I desperately desired to attend became an idol in my life. I didn't realize it until I began writing this book but the desire to attend Spelman College took every place in my heart and I allowed it to be my god. I looked to it for fulfillment, identity and purpose. Not realizing that God was already offering me all of these and more at a free price! But again, in His infinite mercy, I didn't end up attending that school because God knew that if He allowed me to attend Spelman; I would have become just like the Israelites, an idolatrous wife who prostituted His name.

God is a jealous God and He has made it clear all throughout His word that He has a zero tolerance for anything that will serve as an idol in our lives, whether it be school, a relationship, a job, finances, or even your desire for a spouse. Exodus 34:14 says, *"You must worship no other gods, for the LORD, whose very name is Jealous, is a God who is jealous about his relationship with you."* And this jealousy is not motivated by pride or insecurity, as is the case with man. But the Lord is righteous and holy. He is secure within Himself and the jealousy that He has for us says that He will go to extreme measures to protect the honor of His name and those who are in covenant relationship with Him.

God's jealousy is a jealousy that says *"I paid a high price to get you and I will not allow anyone or anything to write me off. You are mine. You belong to me and I will not allow anyone else have you."* This is how valuable we are to Him and it breaks His heart when we allow other things to take the place of our hearts because He knows they can never fulfill us the way that He can.

Often, we count on our academics, relationships, material possessions and social media to "make" us into our own idea of what we think it means to be a man or a woman not knowing that *"Your Maker is your Husband, the LORD Almighty is his name-- the Holy One of Israel is your Redeemer; he is called the God of all the earth."* (Isaiah 45:5). I know that seeing God as a Lover may seem emasculating for men and for women, the whole idea of being known as a Son of God

THE RIGHT TO BECOME

may seem defeminizing but if men can take on a Bridal Identity in Christ then women can take on the role of Sonship.

Our genders are important roles and indicators of how we relate to God and with people, but God does not use our genders to dictate who we are in His Kingdom. If God said that being the Bride of Christ was solely just for women, then that would mean that Jesus only died for women and He didn't. He died for all of humanity. In God's Kingdom your identity precedes your gender. I am not saying that God doesn't care about your gender, He does and if you are a woman then there is a reason why He created you female. If you're a man, there's a reason why He created you male.

Your gender is important and serves a huge role in telling the world who God is both in masculine form and feminine form. Galatians 3:27-28 says, *"And all who have been united with Christ in baptism have put on Christ like putting on new clothes. There is no longer Jew or Gentile, slave or free, male or female. For you are all one in Christ Jesus."*

Trust and believe that the same God who created you is the same God that will make you and mold into the man or woman that He saw before you were even born. He will use your relationships, He will use your family, your pain, your shame, your academics and He may even use that heartbreak that you went through last year but all in all, He will use it and be the one to make you. He's the one who has the stamp of approval over your life so allow Him to be the one who blends all the experiences of your life together to create the unique you. Allow Him to be the one who gets all the glory for your existence. Do not count on these earthly and mundane things to make you. Let the Potter be the Potter. *"And yet, O LORD, you are our Father. We are the clay, and you are the potter. We all are formed by your hand."* (Isaiah 64:8)

THE WOMAN OF MY DREAMS

Ever since I was sixteen years old, I have always had a vision of the type of woman that I wanted to become. This vision was so etched in my mind and engraved in my heart that I sought after it like my entire life depended on it, because in my mind, it did. Everything about this woman intrigued me. Her beauty, her mind, her heart, her passion, her soul...I wanted it all. So, I pursued her, just like Solomon pursued the Shulamite woman.

She was everything that I wanted and aspired to be. The way she walked, the way she talked, the way she composed herself in the most difficult and uncomfortable situations. I saw her beauty; the way her eyes lit up when she smiled, how classy, poised and lady-like she was. I saw her beauty that wasn't solely outward but also inward, you know the type that is so precious to God. I saw her mind; the way she thought deeply and intuitively about things, how she would never settle on just knowing something, but progressed until she knew the who, what, when, where of it all. I saw how she constantly sought-after wisdom, knowledge and understanding in all things. I saw how she chose to be led by the Spirit of God and not by her emotions or feelings. I saw her boldness; her boldness to become everything that Jesus died for her to become and to carry out the Gospel within the ends of the earth. I saw her drive; I saw how determined she was to grow into all that God has called her to be. I saw how she relentlessly pursued her purpose no matter the opposition that came her way.

I saw her passion for God; I saw how deeply she loved Him and wanted to do nothing but bring Him glory and honor. I saw her heart; I saw how compassionate, kind and tenderhearted she was. I saw how she loved much and forgave much because she understood the depth of what was accomplished for her on the cross. I saw her fruit; how loving she was, how joyous she was, how she exudes peace in her life, how patient she was when dealing with all sorts of people, how kind and sincere she was, how she always sought to do good to all men, how gentle and warm her presence was, how faithful and devoted she was to not only to the things of God but to all her commitments a how she always made sure to remind her who was in charge by keeping a disciplined life.

Oh man, I saw her, and I pursued her like she was created to be pursued. I pursued her like God placed the idea of her in my mind knowing that she would someday come in the form of my reality. I pursued her because I knew my future husband, my future children, my family, my friends, all the people that I would be connected to and most importantly my future self, were all depending on me becoming this woman. Not only did I see her, but I *do* see her. Every single day when I wake up I see her.

She's within arm's reach and every single morning I wake up I must make a conscious decision that I am going to become the woman of God that God has called me to be. I don't have to wait for the next big thing to happen in my life. I can be the next big thing. I made up my mind that whatever it takes I must become.

I wanted to be the type of woman that people would look at and say, *"What kind of girl is this?"* I mean the type of woman that men respect, and your little sister aspires to be like. But along the way, in my pursuit of becoming this woman, I realized that I had made it an idol in my life and that this vision was formed out of fear to protect myself.

Protect myself from what? The world. I thought that if I was poised, well-mannered, classy, sophisticated then no man would rob me of the one thing that I could control and that was my femininity. I wanted to control my femininity because I've been hurt by men in my past and I wasn't going to allow myself to get hurt by them again. So, I formulated this vision in my mind and I thought that if I was prim and proper then men wouldn't approach me, they wouldn't gawk at my body like I'm a piece of meat. This was my way of trying to get even with men. But it didn't work because I was also afraid of being a woman and everything that comes with it. When the Lord revealed this to me, I was so surprised because I am the most girliest-girl I know. I love to dress up, get my nails done, wear-makeup, wear heels and do other girly things so my fear of becoming a woman didn't make sense to me.

But the Lord revealed to me that I was afraid of my own beauty, afraid that a man would look at me and think I was beautiful. I was afraid to even know what my body was biologically capable of doing. I was afraid of marriage and the thought of being intimate with my one-day husband. I was afraid of myself. I realized that instead of passionately pursuing this version of a woman in my head, God was calling me to pursue Him and in my pursuit of Him, He would make me become the woman of God that He has called me to be.

Thus, the journey began when I finally realized that my life was not my own and that when I gave my life to Christ, I did just that. I handed my life over to him and completely relinquished any form of control that I had. Galatians 2:20 says, *"My old self has been crucified with Christ. It is no longer I who live, but Christ lives in me. So I live in this earthly body by trusting in the Son of God, who loved me and gave himself for me."* There's this beautiful exchange that happens when Christ died, He gave Himself for me, so now I'll do the same in return, not just one day of my life but for the rest of my life I'll give God my lifetime!

WHAT MAKES A WOMAN...A WOMAN?

I remember asking God one day, *"What makes a woman...a woman? What is the "peak" or the "big arrival" moment of womanhood?"* He responded and said, *"There is no "peak" or big arrival point. You don't step into womanhood; you grow into womanhood."* It's all about growth. A girl doesn't just wake up one morning and become a woman she grows into womanhood and all the experiences that she has faced over the course of her life were all specifically designed to shape, mold, mature and grow her into a woman. There is a seed inside of a woman that has no choice but to grow. That seed was

planted in her before she was even placed in her mother's womb and the moment, she makes her grand entrance into the world she begins her journey

So there you have it ladies, I'm sorry to burst your bubble but there is no defining moment that gives you entry into this beautiful thing called womanhood, you just simply grow into it. Every single day of your life. You grow and you discover, you unravel, and you learn a little more about yourself than you did the day before because if you still have breathe in your lungs then there is still so much depth to you that has yet to be discovered.

What makes a woman a woman are the many trials and tribulations that she has faced through life that she overcame and in turn have allowed them to make her stronger, wiser, braver and more courageous. We are female by birth, but we grow into womanhood. True womanhood is a lifelong journey that I have decided to embark on. Many people today who are well into their 30's, 40's, 50's and even 60's are still little girls trapped in a grown woman's body. Our composition and psyche help us to identity ourselves as woman; however, we are not solely our outward appearance. We are so much more than our hips, breasts, thighs and our curves.

We are grace. We are dignified. We are substance. We are class. We are strength. We are courage. We are beauty. We were created in the image and likeness of the Godhead and we are so precious in the eyes of God. We were created with worth, value, purpose and skill. We are loved. We are adored. We are cherished. We are God's most-prized possession. We are the apple of God's eye. We were bought a high price. We are not to be abused, mistreated, undermined or ridiculed. We are to be treated with respect and honor as daughters of the Most High.

The thought of becoming a woman has always been so intriguing and beautiful to me. I'm so grateful that God decided to make me a female because I know that I get to experience a lot of things that no other gender could. I get the chance to relate to God in such a unique and beautiful way. No, I'm not a feminist but I do believe that there is something beautiful about the female that God created, and I have always desired to seek out her purpose and role in the earth.

Hearing the words "her" and "she" have always greatly affirmed my femininity. Every time someone refers to me using these two pronouns something inside of me lights up and I feel awakened to who I am again. I am "her". I am "she". I am a woman solely after

God's design of womanhood. Society has set a standard on what a woman should look, act, think and talk like but there is standard for godly femininity and that standard can only be found in God's holy world, not in the world.

Whether you are a girl or a boy or a man or a woman reading this book, it's important for you to understand who God has created you to be as a woman or as a man. This understanding of your biological make-up is very key in your process of becoming. And all I am doing is simply just sharing with you all my personal experiences and what I've gleaned from learning what true biblical womanhood looks like.

I have yet to arrive or even to reach my mark in life and I in no way that I have "arrived" but I share these things to tell you that I am growing and becoming. We all are, and it doesn't always look like you're growing while you're growing. It's not until the seed is fully sprouted and the season is over that you look back and realize that hey, you learned a few things. You've made some progress and the person that you are today is not who you used to be.

In my journey of becoming, I have learned that being gentle with myself is one of the hardest things for me to do. I'm my biggest critic. Why? Because I have standards for myself and I have a vision of the type of woman that I want to become so when I do something, say something or act a certain way that does not support this vision I beat myself up. I will literally condemn myself not realizing that the standard that I was using to measure myself with was so weak and flawed. The world will tell you that your only competition should be yourself but Romans 3:23 says *"For everyone has sinned; we all fall short of God's glorious standard."* There is a glorious standard that the Lord wants us to obtain and that standard is not found in this world or even within ourselves, that standard is found in Christ.

I realized that the reason why I kept falling short and condemning myself countless of times was because I was using myself as my own standard of measurement. A standard that was weak, skewed and of carnal.

When you judge yourself using your own standard of measurements, you're always going to end up coming short because you're not perfect. The only viable thing that we should use as our standard of measurement in our journey of becoming is someone that is perfect and incapable of committing error. And that someone is Jesus. Over time, I have learned to stop being the Judge over my own life and understand that my sins have already been atoned for. I've earned to believe the Word of God for what it really is when it says there truly is no condemnation for those who are in Christ Jesus and that when I make a mistake, He's always there to catch me when I fall.

I have also learned that there are no shortcuts to maturity. Growth takes time. The development of Christ-like character cannot be rushed. While I'm worried about how fast I'm growing, God is more concerned with how strong I'm growing and what I'm learning through the process. When it comes to a plant, the farmer is never worried about how fast the seed is growing because He knows that growth for this seedling is inevitable. It was predestined grow. In fact, the very reason why the seed exists is so that it can grow and become something. The farmer is more concerned about whether the seed is getting enough nutrients to aid in its development. Is it getting adequate sunlight and water? Is it in the proper environment it needs to be in? Is it being tended after well?

Everyday God wants us to become a little more like Him. Real maturity is never the result of a single experience no matter how powerful or moving. It is a gradual and continuous process. I heard someone once say, *"Our lives gradually become brighter and more beautiful as God enters our lives and we become more like Him."* This is to say that growth happens overtime and "little by little"

I came to the realization that I was never going to be perfect. Not in this life at least. I had this idea, this image and picture of the type of woman that I wanted to become but I was allowing this vision

THE RIGHT TO BECOME

to become my god. I was limiting God by viewing what He could do through my life through something so abstract. So, the pressure to perform is now off. I can finally breathe. I don't have to strive. I can find freedom and solace in the fact that I will make mistakes, I will fail, I will mess up and I'm not going to make the wisest decisions all the time but the Good News of the Gospel is that *"His grace is sufficient and that His strength is made perfect through my weaknesses."* (2nd Corinthians 12:9).

JOYCELYN OGUNSOLA

5

<u>Into His Marvelous Light</u>

I once heard someone say that *"everyone's much is much to them"* and it reminded me of Ephesians 4:7 which says, *"But to each one of us grace has been given as Christ apportioned it."* God has given us each a measure of grace to handle certain things. There are certain things and situations in life that I don't have the grace to handle and on the other hand there are certain things and situations that God has allotted me the grace to handle. That's why the Bible also tells us that God will never give us more than we can bear. 1st Corinthians 10:13 says, *"We all experience times of testing, which is normal for every human being. But God will be faithful to you. He will screen and filter the severity, nature, and timing of every test or trial you face so that you can bear it. And each test is an opportunity to trust him more, for along with every trial God has provided for you a way of escape that will bring you out of it victoriously."* (The Passion Translation)

The storms, the stretching, the crushing, the pressing, the perplexities of life that came knocking at my door were all granted permission by someone who holds the entire solar system in space; someone who is far bigger and greater than anything that I can ever imagine, someone who's name alone is Sovereign. Though painful, God was the one that allowed me to go through these things not only because He knew that I could handle it but because He knew that the very thing that crushed me was going to produce glory in my life.

A couple years ago, I stopped asking God why He allowed me to go through certain things and began asking Him what were the key lessons that He wanted me to learn during those storms. If God is completely sovereign and in complete control over the entire universe then that means a couple of things: 1. Nothing in my life catches Him by surprise 2. God may sometimes allow bad things to happen to demonstrate His goodness. There are a few examples in the Bible that demonstrate this. Let's take Job's story for example. Job was a man of God who lived in complete uprightness and integrity before the Lord and this man was blessed. He had a wife, beautiful children and multiple businesses that were thriving. Job was living what many would consider today "The American Dream".

One day, Satan, the accuser of the brethren, appeared before the Lord in court patrolling around the earth, seeking for one of God's children to test. But get this...God was the one who brought up Job's name. Job 1: 8-12 *"Have you noticed my servant Job? He is the finest man in all the earth. He is blameless, a man of complete integrity. He fears God and stays away from evil. Satan replied, "Yes, but Job has good reasons to fear God. You have always put a wall of protection around him and his home and his property. You have made him prosper in everything he does. Look how rich he is! But reach out and take away everything he has, and he will surely curse you to your face!" "All right, you may test him," the LORD said to Satan. "Do whatever you want with everything he possesses, but don't harm him physically." So Satan left the LORD's presence."*

Job was considered by God to be put to a test by Satan. This makes me think, people always wonder why do bad things happen to good people? But good people aren't immune to troubles, pain and hardships. Sometimes God tests us just so that he can be glorified. In this story with Job, the joke was on Satan himself, God knew his son. He knew that after Job was tested that he was going to come out looking like pure gold.

Job was being considered because of blamelessness before the Lord. His uprightness was a means for God to promote him to suffering and pain. In the same like-manner, Jesus' uprightness and blamelessness also promoted Him to suffering and pain but at the end of the day (in both circumstances) it was so that the Father would be glorified. Both men had done nothing to deserve that amount of pain that they endured but God saw their innocence to display His glory in their lives. God wasn't playing himself when He asked Satan..." *Have you considered Job my servant?*" God knew exactly what He was doing. While God allowed Satan to test him, He had Satan thinking that He had some control. Ha! The joke was all on him. All authority and power have been given to Jesus then, now and forevermore. God had a plan that involved Him being glorified more in Job's life.

It's funny because the enemy really thought He was in control but after the first chapter we don't hear much of Satan. Instead, we see God's sovereign hand over Job's life being manifested in ways honestly beyond our comprehension. Job went through so much. He lost everything that affirmed his masculinity. He considers committing suicide multiple times, and on top of that his "friends" don't even believe him when he says that he's innocent before the Lord. But in all this Job never turned his back on God. Job just wanted answers. He just wanted to know what He had done to deserve all the agony he was facing.

At the end of the story, what really got me was not that God ended up restoring double of Job's fortunes but in Job 42:5, Job says…"*I have only heard of you before, but now I have seen you with my own eyes.*" So I believe God allowed Job to go through all of this suffering and calamity so that he could taste and see that God is good. I believe that all the questions that God asked Job caused him to realize that he was acquainted with God's hand but not His face. Job knew God as provider because He was a very affluent, rich and prosperous in every way a human being desires to be. But it was only through his suffering that that he was finally able to see God for who He really is; sovereign, almighty, capable and completely in control. I believe that's the greatest miracle of this whole story; that Job was finally able to *see* God and in seeing Him, He was able to know Him.

Job's story is one that makes me sit back and think…what if my whole entire life, every single thing that I've been through, the abuse, the shame, the failures, the pain, the hiding, the insecurity, what if God had me go through all of this so that I can *see* Him? So I that I could *know* Him? What if God knew that the things that I would go through would be so unbearable that I have choice but to go to Him? It's so like God to use the foolish things of the world to confound the wise. He will do anything for His sons to know Him, even if it means having them go through suffering. Why? Because suffering is a prerequisite for glorification.

ALL FOR GLORY

Summer 2016-2017 was the year that I prayed for God's glory more than anything in my life. I so desperately wanted to look and be like Jesus. I wanted to walk like him, talk like him, think like him, interact with him, I wanted *Him*. I would cry out for his glory and pray crazy prayers like *"God, I'll do anything for your glory"* and I can assure you that I had no idea the depth of what I was praying or what it even meant, all I knew was that it felt right. It felt like a prayer that I should be praying and then one day in deep prayer, God said…*"Joycelyn, you know a lot of people cry out for my glory and alot of people want my glory to be made manifest in their lives but they don't want to suffer."*

When the Lord to me this, I didn't understand the magnitude of those words until I went through my own furnace of affliction. And it was in that furnace that I realized that suffering is indeed a prerequisite for glorification. In order to be glorified, you must suffer. You must go through things. This is true of everything. Nothing in life comes easy; not a degree, marriage, getting a new house, writing a book, starting a new business, none of these.

I realized that when we cry out for God's glory, what we're really saying is, *"God I want to fellowship with you in your sufferings, I want to taste your death."* 1st Timothy 2:12 says, *"If we endure/suffer with him, we shall also reign with him."* Take Jesus, our Big Brother, for example, at the Garden of Gethsemane, He was dealing with the weight of carrying all of humanity's sin on his shoulders (including mine and yours) and he didn't want to do it anymore. It was unbearable. It was weighty. But nevertheless, he surrendered to God's will for His life and endured the cross and guess what? He did it for the joy that was set before him because he knew that there was glory awaiting him on the other side. On the cross, where His love ran red, His focal point was you and I. I was His inspiration; I was His personal motivation to continue to press on. He knew that I was on the other side of His obedience. That is why we call Him the pioneer and champion of our faith today. Imagine if Jesus didn't die, if Jesus didn't suffer, we would have never known what life with God would have been like.

None of my pain and suffering was meaningless. It all serves a divine purpose and it's all supposed to produce something great in my life. My weaknesses are a platform for God to show out and for Him to be glorified and that's why I can boldly boast in my weakness because when I am weak then He is strong. Jesus didn't die just so that you and I could be saved. He died so that we could become something. Everything that you have ever gone through in life (and will go through) is supposed to produce an eternal weight of glory. It's your responsibility, as a bride of Christ, a son of God, as an ambassador for the Kingdom of God to make sure that you become everything that

Jesus died for me to become. Make up your mind today that no matter what you've gone throw, that you will become everything that Jesus died for you to become. All of creation is waiting for you and I to step up, take our rightful place in this world and become the version of you that he predestined before he laid the foundations of the world. But do understand that your becoming is going to offend some people as well. It may cost you some relationships; your family may turn their backs against you, and some may even be jealous, and I must be okay with that.

God uses our deepest pains to prune us and to bring about a far greater glory in our lives. That abuse that you went through is going to produce glory. That failure that you experienced is going to produce glory. That sickness, I say to you is not unto death, but it is going to produce glory. That shame and feeling of abandonment is going to produce glory. Everything is going to work together for your good.

So, my dear friend, I hope and pray that the stories that I shared with you encouraged you to get back up. It doesn't matter where you are in life, you can still become. Because He who knew no sin became sin so that you could become something. So take your place, take your seat, lay ahold of what is rightfully yours and become.

————

I want to end this chapter by highlighting one key component to becoming everything that Jesus died for you to become and that is accepting Jesus Christ into your life. John 1:12 says, *"But to as many who have believed him, he gave them the right to become sons of God, even to them that believed in his name."* So if you've made it all the way to the end of this chapter and you have yet to receive Jesus Christ as your Lord and Savior and if you are ready to receive this man that has died for you just so that you could become something that today is your day! Romans 10:9-10 says, *"If you openly declare that Jesus is Lord and believe in your heart that God raised him from the dead, you will be saved. For it is by believing in your heart that you are made right with God, and it is by openly declaring your faith that you are saved."*

If you are ready to become who you already are in Christ Jesus and receive the beautiful gift of salvation, then with all sincerity in your heart, pray this prayer aloud to the God the sees you.

Dear Lord, I believe with my heart that Jesus Christ is Lord and Savior over my life. I repent from all form of sin. I pray that the precious blood of Jesus that you shed on Calvary for sin will make me anew in you. I receive you into my heart now, now give me the grace to become everything that you died for me to become. May your Holy Spirit empower me to live righteously.

In Jesus Name, AMEN.

REFERENCES

New Living Translation Bible

The Passion Translation Bible

ABOUT THE AUTHOR

Joycelyn Ogunsola is a Nigerian-American 23-year-old Author, Writer, Speaker, Influencer and Podcast Host of her new podcast that she just released in July of 2019 titled, "Vulnerable Moments With Jo", where she shares different vulnerable moments of her life with the world in hopes to encourage, inspire and bring hope to the hearts of many. Joycelyn has dedicated the rest of her life to becoming everything that God has called her to be as a Son of God because she lives with an awareness that her life mandates this. She currently lives in Bowie, Maryland with her family and is an active member of her new home church, Glory Center Family Church, Oracles of God Missions located in Largo, Maryland. She enjoys reading, writing, having genuine conversations with people, fellowshipping with her community and helping people in any aspect that she can.

Stay connected with Joycelyn to see what new projects she's working on! Instagram: @joycelynogunsola, Twitter: @JoycelynO_ Podcast page: @vmwithjo, Email: vmwithjo@gmail.com

Made in the USA
Columbia, SC
22 September 2019